9 9400

The
Yellow
Boat

ISBN: 0-8136-5533-1
Printed in the United States of America

  ⁷ 18 19 20 21   06

1-800-321-3106
www.pearsonlearning.com

The
Yellow
Boat

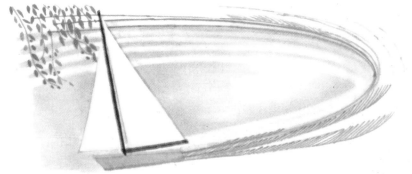

Margaret Hillert

Illustrated by Ed Young

MODERN CURRICULUM PRESS

Look here, look here.

See the little boat.

A little yellow boat.

The boat can go.

It can go away.

Go, little boat, go.

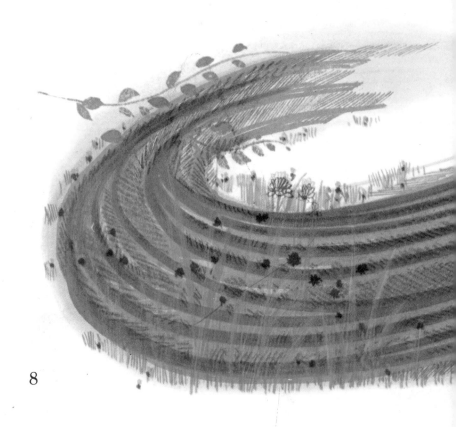

Away, away.

The boat can go away.

Oh, look, look.

Here is something.

It is funny.

Oh, my.

It can jump.

See it jump.

Jump, jump, jump.

Oh, oh, oh.

Something big is here.

Big, big, big.

Can it jump?

It can not jump.

It can go down, down, down.

Look here, look here.

One little one.

Two little ones.

Three little ones.

Where is the boat?

Where is it?

Find the little boat.

Oh, here it is.

Here is the yellow boat.

Go, boat, go.

Go away, away.

Here is something little.

It is blue.

It can go up.

Up, up, up and away.

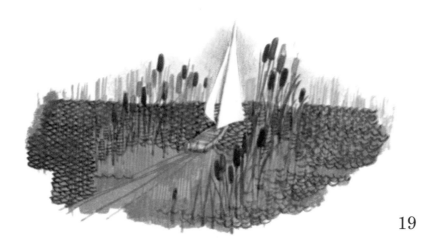

Here is a mother.

Here is a baby.

A little yellow baby.

Look, look.

See the baby play.

And here is something funny.

Help, help.

Go away, go away.

You make me want to run.

Here comes something.

I see something little.

Oh my, oh my.

It is a little yellow boat.

See the yellow boat.

Oh, yellow boat.

I want you.

I want you.

Come to my house.

Here you go.

In here, in here.

Go, yellow boat, go.

MCP Beginning-to-Read Books

Uses of these books. These books are planned for the very youngest readers, those who have been learning to read for about six to eight weeks and who have a small preprimer reading vocabulary. The books are written by Margaret Hillert, a first-grade teacher in the Royal Oak, Michigan, schools. Each book is illustrated in full color.

Children will have a feeling of accomplishment in their first reading experiences with these delightful books that *they can read.*

The Yellow Boat

Children will enjoy the adventure of the yellow boat which is charmingly illustrated and uses just 43 preprimer words.

Word List

7 look	funny	baby
here	**11** my	**21** play
see	jump	**23** help
the	**12** big	you
little	**13** not	make
boat	down	me
a	**14** one	want
yellow	two	to
8 can	three	run
go	**15** where	**24** comes
it	find	I
away	**18** blue	**26** house
10 oh	**19** up	**27** in
is	and	
something	**20** mother	